Jake is a Big Brother

Story by Charles LaBelle

www.jakestories.com
Illustration by Jake Stories Publishing
Children's stories and Jake's Brain Training Games

Jake Stories Publishing
Children's stories and Jake Brain Training Games

www.jakestories.com
© 2015 Charles J. LaBelle

National Library of Canada Cataloguing in Publishing Data
LaBelle Charles J.

Story by Charles Labelle
Illustration by Jake Stories Publishing
Jake is a Big Brother

ISBN 978-1-896710-54-9

Jake is a Big Brother

Jake felt angry, he thought, *this isn't good.*

His classmates teased his friend Cole.
"You're a chicken, Cole!" they shouted.

"You're too scared to climb the giant pine tree at Mr. Tiller's.
You can't do it."

"Yes, I can," shouted Cole. "I'll do it Saturday; tomorrow at ten a.m."

Jake ran to stand by Cole, and raised Cole's hand above his head.

Jake shouted, "Cole and I will climb the scary pine tree, right up to the
Gotcha-bird's cave nest, and bring back a feather."

Cole shouted, "I'm not afraid of the Gotcha-bird.
And if you're not afraid of the Gotcha-bird, come and watch us!"

Saturday morning was wet and dark. Jake waited for Cole at Mr. Tiller's. He looked up at the giant pine tree. Strong wind blew rain into his face. It stung his cheeks and turned them red.
He tried to see the top of the scary giant pine tree but it was hidden by mist.

The branches were as far apart as the distance between Jake's dad's toes and Jake's dad's head. There were a hundred branches to climb to reach the Gotcha-bird nest.

Jake thought, *No turning back now.*
Cole and I must do it today. This is a perfect day.
A stormy day is the day the Gotcha-Bird will stay in his cave nest.

Jake felt scared when he looked up at all those branches.

He remembered that the high school kids said,
"Gotcha-birds eat little boys and poop them out in piles of bones."

Jake said he didn't believe them, but maybe he did; just a little bit.

Jake liked the Gotcha-birds even though they had red eyes, spat fire, and sometimes pooped on your head. He'd show those school bullies that he and Cole could climb right up to the Gotcha-bird's cave nest.

While Jake waited, a bunch of his classmates arrived.
Even some high school kids turned up. They shouted,
"Where's that chicken, Cole?"

Jake was worried, *Did Cole change his mind? What if I have to climb the tree all alone?* Jake's stomach began to ache. *What if I slip in bird poo and fall? Everyone will laugh at me!*

Finally Cole stumbled out of the mist looking pale and miserable.

His sister's Emma and Sarah were right behind him. They shouted, "Wait Cole, we don't want you to climb the scary pine tree. We don't want you to meet the Gotcha-bird. We don't want you to hurt yourself."

Jake shouted, "Come on, we can do this!" He jumped for the first branch. It was much too high.

He and Cole jumped and stretched again and again.
Each time, they fell back to the ground.

"Boo, boo! Can't do it!" yelled the crowd.

Jake jumped up from the mud and helped Cole to his feet.
He raised Cole's arm in the air.
Sarah and Emma rushed over and raised Cole's other hand.

"Yes he can do it!" shouted Jake and Emma and Sarah.

Then a wonderful thing happened.
Everyone joined in and shouted, **"Yes he can!"**

Jake made a step with his knee. Cole jumped from Jake's knee.
His hands grabbed the first branch and he swung his leg over.

"Hooray!" yelled the crowd.

Emma made a step with her knees for Jake.
Jake ran forward, jumped off her knees, and flew onto the first branch.

He shouted, **"Ouch!"** as he landed on his stomach.

Cole moved his hands up the trunk of the tree.

They slipped on Gotcha-bird poo.

He fell turning a summersault in the air.
His head bumped on the ground.

Everyone gasped,
"Ohhhh no!

Cole, are you hurt?

Is that Gotcha-bird poo on your hands?

Yuck, yuck.
Does it
stink?"

Cole lay still. Cole didn't answer.

Cole was remembering a dream that he had last night.

In the dream, he could float as high as the roof of his house by concentrating with all his might.

Cole sat on the ground, closed his eyes, and thought real hard.

There was a whistle in the air.
Then as quick as you could say "Spider-Man,"
he was on top of the first branch.

Cole sat there, right on some Gotcha-bird poo, and thought real hard.
"It works!" he shouted.
Now he was on the second branch.

Jake and Cole shouted,
"Only ninety-eight more branches!"

The crowd cheered,
"Hooray! Go Cole! Go

And then they all stopped cheering.
Even Jake, Emma, and Sarah stopped. Everyone looked very puzzled.
They all asked each other, "How did he do that?"
But nobody knew.

Jake wished he could float. It was hard work to climb such a big tree.

Jake thought,
I can't let Cole go on alone. I must stay with my friend no matter what.

He climbed faster to keep up, hand over hand, branch after branch.

Cole continued thinking hard and floating.
Finally they were both sitting right next to the Gotcha-bird cave nest.
They were both very tired, especially Jake.
His arms and legs ached.
His heart beat fast.
He couldn't see the ground.
He couldn't see anyone in the rain.

Jake thought,
But I can still hear everyone still asking questions.

"How did you do that? Are you all right? Can you see us?
We can't see you.
Can you see the Gotcha-bird?

Jake and Cole didn't answer.
They were at the entrance to a big cave made of branches.

Suddenly Gotcha-bird poked his head out of the cave.
He opened his huge red eyes.
He yawned a big, red fiery yawn that burnt the shoelaces right out of
Cole's shoes.

The smoke made Jake's eyes itchy and he coughed and sneezed.

Gotcha-bird stretched his wings over Jake and Cole's heads.
They sat on their branch, shaking.

Suddenly Cole remembered Jake saying, *'Cole and I will climb the
scary pine tree, right up to the Gotcha-bird cave-nest, and bring back
a feather.'* He remembered the cheers of the crowd.
Cole took a big breath and remembered his new powers.
He thought real hard about a big bird with no fire.

Gotcha-bird's fire went out.
"Hey! How did you do that?" asked Gotcha-bird.

Cole thought real hard again. He thought about himself and Jake sitting on Gotcha-bird's back.

They floated up onto Gotcha-bird's back and held on to the edge of his fluffy green ears.

Gotcha-Bird asked, "Hey, how did you do that?"

"I'll show you how if you'll be our friend," said Cole.

"OK," said Gotcha-bird,
"I don't have any friends, so that would be cool."

"Will you promise not to eat us up and poop us out into a little pile of bones?" asked Jake.

The big bird laughed; big long laughs, with puffs of smoke.
"I don't eat anyone,
I eat grass nuts and berries," he said.

"I'm glad," said Cole. "Can we see your cave nest?"

"Come right in," said the bird.

They climbed off and went into Gotcha-bird's cave nest.
It was a magic cave, small on the outside but bigger than Jake's house on the inside. How come your cave nest looks so small outside but it's so big inside?" asked Cole.

"Different dimension," said Gotcha-bird.

"Oh wow that's cool!" said Jake.

Gotcha-Bird had a swimming pool, a skateboard, Lego sets, video games, video movies, soccer balls, game cards, checker sets and stacks and stacks of Spider Man comics.
Gotcha-Bird had all the things that the boys loved to play with.

The boys were happy because they had a new friend.

Cole taught Jake and Gotcha-bird how to think hard.

He taught them to think hard and make things happen.

. . .

Cole got really tired thinking and teaching.

Jake asked Gotcha-bird,
"Could you fly us home?
Our thinkers are really tired."

Gotcha-bird smiled and replied,
"I'd love to."

They sat on the big bird's back and held on to his fluffy green ears.

Gotcha-bird flew down through the tree branches and the mist.

The boys flew into the crowd on the Gotcha-Bird's back.

Everyone went,

"Aaaaaaa! Oh! Wow!"

Cole shouted so Jake could hear him,
"I couldn't have done it without your help Jake.
You were like a big brother to me."

Jake shouted into the wind . . .

"I knew you could do it.
I'll be your big brother any time you want."

Everyone wanted to touch Gotcha-bird's green fluffy ears.
He let them as long as they didn't try to pull any feathers
out.

Everyone even Big Bad Bill was gentle with Gotcha-bird.

Gotcha-bird gave one big green feather to Cole before he left.
Cole told Jake they could share it.

Gotcha-bird flew back into the big tall pine tree.
He flew into his cave-nest in the other dimension.

Everyone shouted,
"Hooray Gotcha-bird didn't poop on us!"

**The children knew why he was called
Gotcha-bird.**

**They knew that that he sometimes pooped on your
head and said, "Gotcha."**